The Day Santa Came

By

Stephen Dignall

McStay

This book is dedicated to the magic that is Christmas.

It's the night before Christmas, the omens are grave, for giving my children the yuletide they crave.
With so little money how can we survive? It's breaking my heart that my kid's must deprive.

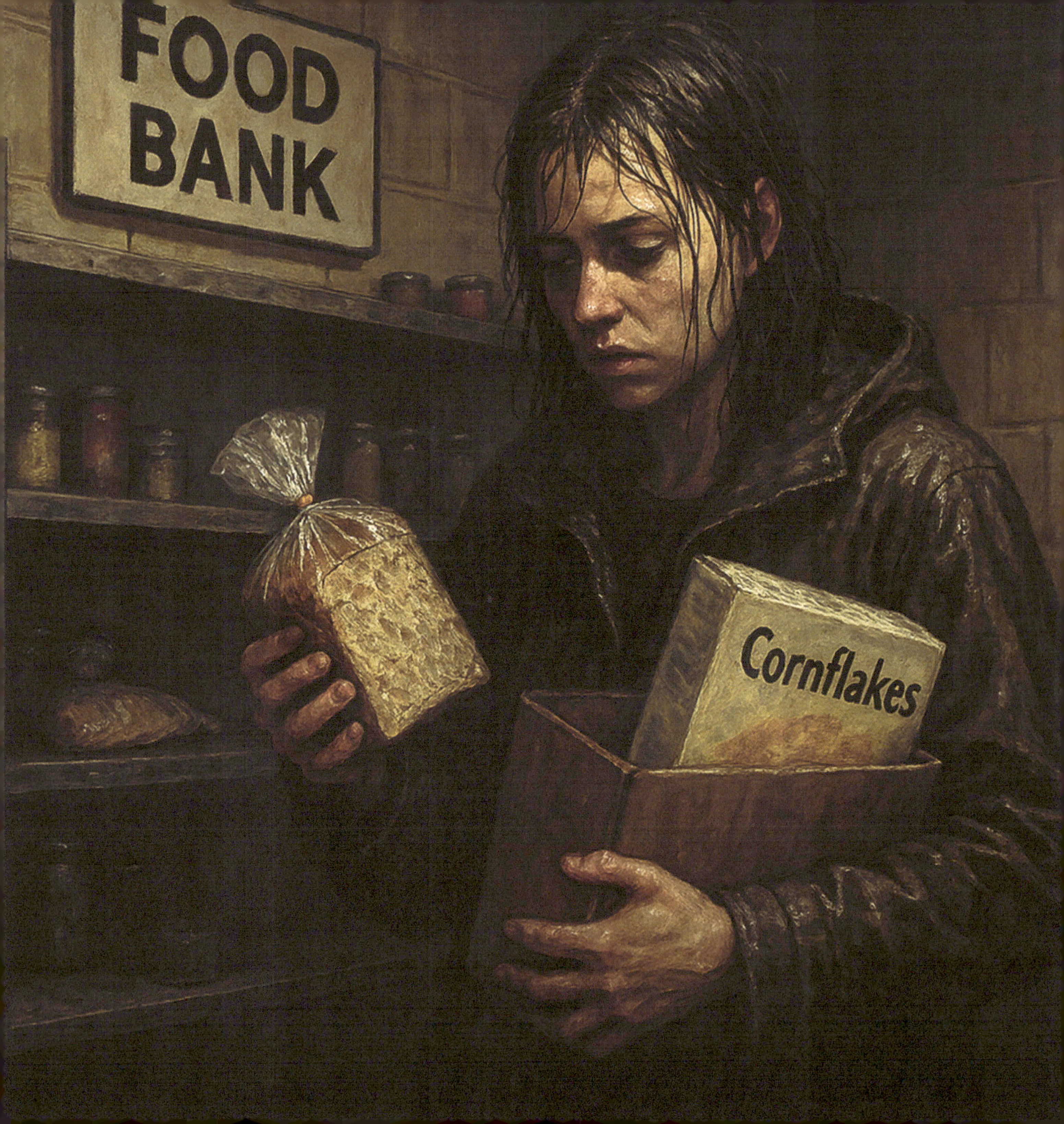
FOOD
BANK
Cornflakes

I went to the food bank, there wasn't much there, just stale bread and cornflakes, I left in despair.
The kids are excited, for what I can't say. They both believe Santa is coming their way.

With the rent overdue and bills to be paid, I pray that tomorrow might just be delayed. How can I give them the day they desire, the TV is broken, it's all looking dire. I've spent all my time just walking the streets, hoping to find them some bargains and treats.

It's now getting dark and I still haven't eaten, I'm wet and I'm cold, but refuse to be beaten.
The Superstore carpark is starting to empty, just the right time to find bargains aplenty.

I look on the shelves, there isn't much left, 'cept two scrawny turkey's forlorn and bereft. They've been on the shelf now for over a week, they're bound to reduce them, they're well past their peak

Here comes the assistant, price labeller in hand, to mark down those turkey's once they have been scanned. He picks up the birds, putting them on his trolley, I just hope and pray that I've got enough lolly.

Keeping my eyes firmly fixed on the prize, a £1 for the turkey, now that's a surprise!
'Can I have that turkey?' I say, loud and clear.
'Not till I say so,' he snaps with a sneer.

I patiently stand contemplating my fate, I'm sure he's deliberately making me wait. My heart is now pounding, it's getting quite late. This type of jobsworth I specially hate.

'Why can't I have one, you've just marked them down?'
'There's rules to be followed,' he says with a frown.

Getting frustrated, I finally break, and start to berate this cold-hearted snake.
'I need to get back to my kids,' I sob.
'It's no good you crying, just doing my job.'

'I don't want to feed them on Twizzlers,' I sighed. 'I may be hard-up, but I've still got my pride.' Ignoring my plea, like a grumpy old elf, places one on the racking, takes one for himself.

An elbow, a shoulder, a scramble, a scrap. Hands grabbing turkey, my chances elapse.
In the midst of the scuffle I'm knocked to the floor. Defeated, dejected, my tears start to pour.

I leave empty-handed and trudge throught the snow. The bus is due shortly, the North wind doth blow.

I see in the distance, bus waiting in line. I make a mad dash; I'm cutting it fine.

Breathless and panting I stand and I fume, as I watch the tail-lights fading into the gloom, the last bus has gone, I have to walk home. I'm aching and shivering, chilled to bone.

I finally arrive, only to see, two kids at the window watching for me.

'It's baked beans on toast,' I cheerfully shout, to moans and groans from two hungry mouths. The kids are excited, it's Christmas Eve, each of them wondering what Santa will leave.

A carrot for Rudolph, mince pie for St Nick, I hope when they eat them they don't make them sick.

I give them a bath, and put them to bed, then slump on the sofa, my heart filled with dread. It's too cold to sit with no TV or heat, so under the blankets I'm forced to retreat.

Later that night, I have a strange dream, Santa, his helpers, and reindeers have been.

I wake up next morning, only to hear, my children's laughter so loud and so clear. How come they're so so happy, playful and jolly, sat in a cold house with no tree or Holly?

My room door flies open, they're merry and gay, 'Come down and see what he's brought us today.'

I follow them down, and to my disbelief; a Christmas tree, fairy lights, present's beneath.

A warm fire is burning, we've got a new Telly, everywhere's piled high with cakes, sweets, and jelly

'Come into the kitchen,' one of them shouts, 'the carrot and mince pie have turned into sprouts. Sat on the table, to my great surprise, a large Christmas feast to gladden the eyes.

Sleigh-bells are jingling, who's at the back door? Hoof marks and footprints lie fresh on the floor

I gaze to the heavens, and high overhead, a strange-looking craft, all shiny and red. Is it a mirage, or is it a dream? I look up again, but there's nought to be seen.

As long as I live, I will never explain, exactly what happened The Day Santa Came.

www.ingramcontent.com/pod-product-compliance
Lightning Source LLC
Chambersburg PA
CBHW041002170626

46815CB00002B/119